MW00834650

Sex Stories for Adults

An Erotica Collection of Explicit Taboo Encounters Full of Threesomes, Spanking, BDSM, Hardcore Anal, Cuckold, Orgasmic Oral, First Time Lesbian, Naughty 365 Days, and More.

Samantha Lexi

Copyright © 2022 by Samantha Lexi

All rights reserved.

It is not legal to reproduce, duplicate, or transmit any part of this document in either electronic means or in printed format. Recording of this publication is strictly prohibited and any storage of this document is not allowed unless with written permission from the publisher except for the use of brief quotations in a book review.

This book is a work of fiction. Any resemblance to persons, living or dead, or places, events, or locations is purely coincidental.

Contents

♥

Sand in Awkward Places

❝ W hat are you thinking?" Gregor laughed at Ariel as she watched a group of hard bodies strut down the beach.

She rolled, lifting her shoulders from the towel, exposing her ample breasts.

"I'm thinking many things," she practically purred. "Firstly, I was thinking that it might be time for more tanning oil. Then I was distracted by those pretty men. I wondered if I should call out to one of them to help me, since you are ignoring me, tucked up under that umbrella. Then I thought that the blonde was going to have quite the sunburn. His chest is starting to look pink."

"I'm hardly ignoring you, my love, I'm simply doing my part to avoid skin cancer."

"And I'm courting it," she retorted.

"But it looks so good on you. You, yourself, have mentioned how much my winter white paleness is a better aesthetic for me."

Gregor ran a well-manicured hand across one cheek and down his chest. He was frosty pale with the blackest hair and red lips. He looked more like he belonged in a vampiric castle, wearing ruffled shirts and pants everyone referred to as breeches, than he did out on the beach.

"Do you want to play with them?" he asked.

"Can I?" Ariel sat on her hip, facing him. With her breasts now fully exposed, the brown nipples peaked as she looked at him. He was beautiful, and she did appreciate the contrast of his paleness against her tanned skin.

"Well? Are you going to rub me down or not?"

"I think not."

Ariel squealed indignantly, "You're being unfair." She began throwing sand around.

"Do you need some help, here?" A deep voice caught their attention.

Gregor looked up from where his wife was throwing a fit to a trio of firm, tan young studs. The blond his wife mentioned earlier was standing in front of his friends. The tops of his pecs were highlighted in the tell-tale pink of a raging sunburn, as were the top curves of his broad shoulders. He smirked with confidence.

His friends had slightly less composure as they openly stared at Ariel's display of glorious breasts.

"Why yes, I believe we could use your assistance," Gregor replied.

The three men stepped closer as Ariel lifted up a bottle of tanning oil. "I need this rubbed on my back."

Gregor's cock began throbbing with anticipation.

The blonde took the bottle from Ariel's hand and knelt next to her in the sand. She laid back down and shifted to get comfortable.

"What's your name?" She asked.

"I'm Zac," he said as he poured oil into his palm and began smoothing it over her back.

"Brian," "Names Jay," said the other two.

Ariel made an uncomfortable grunt and shifted. "Jay, come here." She waved him over. "This sand, it's just not working. Come. Come."

Gregor stretched his legs out and crossed his ankles. His trunks bulged with his growing erection. This was going to be quite the display.

Ariel positioned Jay in front of her so that her chest draped across his lap. "That's so much better," she cooed.

"Uh, yeah." The man's gulp was audible.

Gregor imagined Jay's erection was about to launch itself, it stood so tall. Jay fidgeted and tried to reach Ariel.

"Stop moving," Ariel cooed, "that's perfect." She rubbed her chest into his lap.

She turned to glance up at Zac, who seemed to be rubbing oil into one spot on her back.

Reaching behind, she hooked her fingers into the scraps of fabric that made up her bikini bottoms.

"I hate tan lines. Will you help me take these off?"

"Ah, yeah," Zac didn't seem to know how to respond.

Gregor chuckled at the other men's discomfort. They had tried to be intimidating to get a glimpse of his wife's boobs, and now, well, she was toying with them.

Zac pulled the bottoms down Ariel's legs, and she squired even more.

"Ew, sand. You in the red shorts. Oh, it looks like you brought Mr. Happy to see me."

He quickly grabbed his crotch and began to turn away.

"Don't you dare. You're Brian, right? I have a job for you. Protect me from all this sand."

"What?"

Arial twisted, exposing almost everything, to look up at him. "I need you to be my towel."

Gregor chuckled and handed out a clean towel. "Here you go."

Brian's wide eyes cast from Zac to Jay in an unvoiced question. Jay's eyes were rolling up into his head, he nodded.

"Just do it, man," Zac bit out in a gruff voice.

Brian spread out the fresh towel and laid down, propping his face on folded arms.

"Don't be such a prude," Ariel complained. "Rollover."

She yanked Brian's shorts down his thighs and covered his body with hers before he had time to react.

"So much better," she purred. She shifted around until Brian let out a low moan.

Gregor's hand reached into his shorts and he gripped his shaft. The fun had begun in earnest. She had one of them conquered.

Ariel shifted onto her knees, with her back arched. She was obviously impaled on the man beneath her.

"Where did you go Zac?" she asked. "I still need lotion."

"Yeah right." Zac knelt over Brian's legs so he could reach Ariel's back.

"No, honey." She grabbed his wrists and put his hands on her ass. "Here. Don't be shy. Get oil everywhere."

Gregor reached for another bottle of his wife's lotion and filled his palm. He shoved his trunks out of the way, exposing his pale cock to the air. He rubbed oil over himself, cock and balls before he began stroking in time to Ariel's rocking.

"Jay, I'm feeling exposed," she said as she cupped her boobs, lifting them toward him.

Jay reluctantly got to his feet. She reached out and as she gripped his waistband to drag him closer, she also pulled his shorts down. His cock stood at attention, long and hard. It bounced as blood pulsed into it.

"Perfect," Ariel cooed.

She wrapped her hands around Jay's ass cheeks and pulled his throbbing member to her breasts. Jay's hands went to her breasts as he began thrusting against her.

"Zac, I'm going to need some of that oil up here," she said.

"Yes, ma'am," Zac said.

Ariel let out a long, satisfied moan as Zac poured oil over her and Jay squeezed her boobs and thrust against her. She began lowering and rising up and down against Brian's hips and up into Jay's.

She reached behind her and waved her hand around as if looking for something. Zac put his shaft in her hand.

"She has an empty asshole, Zac," Gregor called out. "You know what to do."

Following Gregor's coaching, Zac reached down and fingered the pucker of Ariel's ass. He slid a finger in.

She screamed, and suddenly the throbbing pulsing mass of bodies all moved as one. Down and up, back and forth. Gregor could barely keep up with his stroking as he watched. Each gasp, each moan drove his hand faster.

"That's it," he said encouragingly. Make sure she is good and fucked.

Ariel looked over her shoulder at him, a wicked smile on her face. She bit her plump lower lip and flicked her tongue at her husband.

She pressed down against his cock. At the same time, she pushed hard against Zac's finger in her ass. She pulled Jay's butt cheeks apart as she gripped him to her breasts.

She bit at Gregor. "Give me something to suck on darling," she begged.

Unable to resist her and the throbbing pulsations of the bodies all pressed against hers, he stood and braved the sun. She latched onto his cock like a starving woman, sucking him down.

From the sounds, Brian was the first one to blow.

Ariel moaned around Gregor. He wrapped a hand around the back of her head and held her to him as he shot his load down her throat. She swallowed. The action was as tantalizing on his cock as it was to watch other men fuck her, outside, under the sun.

He stepped back and Ariel licked the tip of him as she released her hold.

She shifted her mouth from him, and pulling back from Jay fucking her breasts, she clamped her mouth around Jay's member.

Jay gasped and a moment later was fucking her mouth as if he were in the final stretch of a marathon.

Zac took advantage of the shift in positions and pulled Ariel's hips off of the exhausted Brian. Zac sank his shaft deep into Ariel's pussy as it still dripped with Brian's cum.

Gregor returned to his lounge under the sun umbrella. "Oh, that's it, gentlemen. You have her now."

His dick pulsed as if it wanted another go at it.

Jay shouted as he lost, or maybe it was won, his battle against Ariel's mouth. She made a groan deep in her throat, and Gregor watched her throat bounce in such a lovely fashion as she sucked Jay dry.

Zac was the last man fucking. He continued to thrust into Ariel, even as she lay back against his chest, limp as orgasms wracked her body and she was helpless against the muscle spasms. He took a double hand full of her breasts and pounded into her from the back, suddenly cheered on by his friends and Gregor. They were invested in Zac's ability to cum.

When it happened, Ariel found the energy to cry out as Zac filled her. The other men cheered as if they were watching a football game and their team just won the final touchdown.

Ariel rolled off the man's diminishing erection. She pointed to a random spot on her ribs. "I think you missed a spot."

Zac reached up as if he had no energy to move. He swiped his fingers through the cum dripping from her pussy and spread it over her.

"You know darling," Ariel said as she stood and brushed sand from her body. "I think I'm done with the beach. I get sand in the most awkward of places. Shall we go shopping in Monte Carlo next?"

Gregor held out his hand to Ariel and they walked away.

"Dude, what just happened?" Zac asked with a groan.

Jay sat in the sand with a thump. "I think we just got fucked over by the rich."

Tits Out for Turbulence

Dana's stomach leaped to her throat as the plane dipped and shook. She wanted to scream, cry, or panic in some visual way. Her fingers bit into the armrests of her seat. Her eyes darted around the cabin. No one else seemed to notice. They were all calm.

The woman across the aisle from her read a book as if nothing was more interesting. The man in the row behind her had earbuds in. The man in front of her slept. He would occasionally snore, but nothing ever woke him up. The cabin was mostly quiet. What did they know that she didn't?

Dana slid the little window cover-up and looked out. There was nothing to see, they were surrounded by dark gray cotton fluff of clouds. A sudden flash of lightning in the distance illuminated the clouds purple and black.

A warm presence behind her alerted her to her air host's presence. His arm came around from behind and he slid the window shut. "That's not going to help if you're a nervous flier. It's only going to freak you out more."

He leaned into her space and stayed there much longer than he needed to. She wasn't complaining. He was hot, and he smelled nice.

She nodded and sucked in a ragged breath, trying to steady her nerves. Instead what ended up happening was she pushed her boobs against his arm.

She froze as soon as she realized what she had done. Neither of them moved. Her shocked wide eyes looked at his arm in front of her and then up to his face.

He had one of those half-smile, sexy little smirks on his face.

"Sorry," she finally managed. Yet, she still hadn't lowered her boobs. If anything she was arching her back even more.

Slowly, obviously, he slid his arm back letting his hand palm first one breast and then the other. "How about I bring you a glass of wine? You let me know if you need a little distraction if the storm gets to be too much. Okay?"

He righted himself, winked at her, and continued walking up toward the front of the plane. She leaned over the empty seats to watch his ass in those tight uniform pants.

Did he mean what she thought he meant? A mile-high distraction?

The plane did another one of its roller-coaster-like dips. Something went bump in the overhead compartment. The man in front of her snorted, sat upright, and then shifted right back to sleep. The woman with the book looked up. She nodded when they made eye contact, but immediately went back to her book.

Dana swallowed hard and closed her eyes. She focused on her breathing. For some reason, this made her think about pushing her boobs up and pressing against the air host's arm.

Someone sat in the aisle seat and lowered the tray table between them. She opened her eyes to see her hot air host smirking at her. A glass of red wine with a plastic wrap cover and a straw on the table.

"I thought you might want this," he said. "Immediately." His nostrils flared and he gave her one of those looks that felt like a touch. He licked his lips when his eyes paused on her breasts.

He reached out and squeezed her thigh, letting his fingers trail up between her legs. She shuddered when his fingers traced the seam between her legs. He lifted his arm and languidly ran a finger around the call button. He practically caressed it. He pinched and rubbed his fingers over the button and she felt it in her nipples. He wasn't being subtle.

"You know what to do with this, right?"

She gulped. "I press it."

"Right." He nodded. "You press it when you want me."

"Oh, that's how it works?"

He nodded.

Not taking her eyes off him, she leaned into him reached over, and pressed the call button.

He growled low in his throat. "Drink your wine." He stood, flicked the call button off, and walked away.

She popped the straw through the plastic wrap, like an adult juice box, and started sucking down the wine. She kept watching him move down the aisle and she pressed the call button again.

He looked over his shoulder at her and winked.

She sat back in her seat and continued to suck on the straw until her glass was empty.

With incredible timing, her air host was back. He fingered the call button off. He made the action tantalizing and sexually charged.

"Come with me." He held his hand out.

She slid out of her seat and followed him past the bulkhead, and into the back of the plane. He kicked open the door to one of the bathrooms and pulled her in.

The door closed with a click. That was her clue.

He reached for the buttons of her blouse as she scrambled at his belt. Her nipples peaked to attention as soon as the cool air hit her thin bra. He yanked down the thin cup fabric and sucked her into his mouth. It was hot and wet. His tongue ran circles around her nipple. Making her moan.

The plane dipped, and he sucked harder, kneading her other boob with a big hand.

Distracted by his mouth on her, she forgot about undoing his pants. Instead, she pushed her yoga pants down and kicked one leg free. She squirmed her underwear down and hiked her leg around his hips.

His hand abandoned her tit and he found her exposed pussy.

He sucked harder on the nipple in his mouth. He was going to leave a mark. She didn't care. She fumbled with his fly more as he fingered into her cunt.

Suddenly his cock was free. It felt heavy and thick. She wrapped her hand around his hot shaft and pulled him toward her needy hole.

The plane dipped.

She gasped. The seatbelt light pinged on. He shoved into her, and she no longer cared if the plane was experiencing turbulence.

He banged her against the small sink. She was going to have a weird bruise on her ass. But she didn't care. His thick dick slid with glorious friction. He slammed into her so hard his balls bounced against her ass, and his crisp pubic hair brushed her clit.

She held his head hard to her boob. She wanted him to suck all of her in. She shoved her hips at him, wanting more of his cock.

She couldn't tell if it was him or the turbulence. Her stomach felt like it dropped again, and her ears popped from the force of his fucking. He let go of her nipple with a pop.

The captain's voice came over the intercom, "Crew, begin preparing the cabin for landing."

"You're—" thrust— "going to—" thrust— "have to return—" the air host slammed harder into her. He reached between them and flicked her clit— "to your seat. We're descending."

She gasped. He pinched and thrust and fucked her until she couldn't breathe. She wanted to scream as she started to cum. He thrust fingers into her mouth. She sucked on his fingers as he fucked her and she came hard. Explosions in her head left her limp.

He unloaded and she felt his warm cum shoot into her. They pressed together twitching and throbbing for the briefest moment.

He lowered her leg, tucked his tumescent cock back into his pants. Reaching behind her, he washed his hands.

"I have to go back to work. You were done with that wine right?"

And then she was alone in the small bathroom, half undressed with cum leaking down her leg. She cleaned up and returned to her seat.

The man in front was still asleep. She leaned over and grabbed his shoulder and shook. "Harold. Damn it, Harold, wake up. The plane is landing."

He blinked up at her and rubbed his all too familiar face. "All ready? That was a short flight."

As she departed, the attractive air host waved and said, "I hope you had a pleasant flight Mr. and Mrs. Pool."

"Good flight, great job," Harold mumbled.

"Yes, thank you. Very satisfying."

Cum on Periwinkle

♥

Mistress appreciated how the custom-made periwinkle blue vinyl bodysuit perfectly matched the color of the nitrile gloves she snapped on. It was as if the color matching material had been created in the same dye lot.

Her favorite vinyl specialist had outdone themselves with this one. Even the hood, with its imperceptible mesh inlays for breathing, the iridescent rainbow lenses all blended perfectly. With the hood zipped no one could tell what she looked like. The only identifiable feature was her shape. Really, how many people could identify someone by their shape corseted into vinyl alone?

She snapped shiny black patent leather cuffs over the seam where gloves met suit.

With a twist, she opened a tall slender bottle of oil. A smirk crossed her lips, not that anyone could see. The oil added a sheen of extra shine to her body. She poured oil into her palm and coated her arms and torso. Tonight she was going to be as slick as a human slip and slide.

The heels of her thigh-high black boots made a nearly imperceptible clicking sound, as she left her chamber for the viewing room. She tapped a riding crop in a counter beat against her thigh, all while twirling the fringed leather tassel that hung the handle.

The men were already waiting for her arrival. Shirtless, in dark boxer briefs, they all waited in perfect supplication. Each one knelt on the floor, sitting back on their heels, posture upright, hands resting on thighs. Their eyes were trained a foot in front of them on the floor so that their gaze would fall on her feet when she stood in front of them. Collars of studded leather adorned each neck, waist, and wrists with connector chains linking the collars. And a lovely line of erections tented up the front of their shorts.

She appreciated the variety of her choices to select from. Seven men of assorted heights, skin coloring, and build waited for her pleasure.

"Mistress," the keeper of the room greeted her.

Mistress eyed the keeper. Maybe Mistress would shun the men selected for her and take the keeper back to her chamber for playtime. The woman was lithe with delicate features. The piercings along the rim of her ear made it appear as if they came to Elvin little points. Clever jewelry design. Her clothes were barely more than wisps of fabric, hiding nothing underneath. The iridescent blue nipples and blue at the V or her legs displayed a creative use of body makeup.

The blue was almost a perfect match to Mistress's new suit. She gave the long fall of the black ponytail that emerged from the top of her hood a toss as she chuckled to herself. Playing with the help could come later. And she would make the lively little sprite cum, and cum again.

Increasing the slap of the crop against her leg, Mistress strode down the line in front of her choices. Brilliant green eyes darted up from the floor to look at her face. She snapped her gaze around to catch the miscreant, but his eyes were already returned to the floor. A charming little blush pinkened his cheeks. He had been caught, and he knew it.

She turned on her heel and stepped back in front of him. He was well defined, and the promise of that erection intrigued her. She was in the mood for some punishing tonight. With the crop placed under his chin, she lifted his face so she could get a better look at him. Dark waving hair, a dangerous glint in those green eyes. He was either a switch, playing games, or a brat who could not be tamed into complete submission. Either way, he would do.

"This one," she announced.

As she strode out the door, she caught the keeper of the room by one of the ribbons of cloth she adorned herself with. Mistress wound the fabric around her hand, drawing the other woman close.

"You aren't wearing a collar," Mistress purred and caressed the other woman's ass. "Have you been misplaced?"

"I'm feral. I bite," the young woman said.

"I'll keep that in mind." Mistress ran her cheek over and around the other woman's, like a cat rubbing its scent on a favorite person.

Back in her playroom, her selected boy toy of the evening stood awaiting her pleasure. His hands were bound, and he held them clasped together.

"What do I call you?" she asked.

"You can call me Thomas. What do I call you?" The green of his eyes flashed dangerously.

"You call me Mistress. You do not speak unless spoken to, and you do not question me. Clear?"

He cocked an eyebrow up and tilted his head in the slightest of nods.

Her crop lashed out and she struck him across the ass.

He flinched.

"The correct response is—"

"Yes, Mistress." Thomas sounded bored.

Ignoring him - clearly, he was a brat - Mistress examined a display of accouterments and lotions. Tonight she was interested in the personal touch. Or as personal as one could get through three millimeters of vinyl. She grabbed a bottle of lubricant.

She handed it to Thomas.

"Disrobe and rub down with this."

With barely a shrug, Thomas kicked off his shorts and began slathering the lube all over his body.

Mistress watched his hands trail over the dark hairs of his chest. Her mouth began watering as she watched his hands roam down over his abs. The bastard bypassed his growing erection and began rubbing the lotion into his feet.

When she let her gaze return to his face, a mischievous grin played across his lips. He knew exactly what he was doing. The brat.

Mistress turned and grabbed a different lube from the display. She pulled his hand away from his foot, causing him to stumble. She squeezed a palmful of the viscous lotion in his hand and pressed his hand to his cock.

He gasped and pulled his hand away quickly.

"Rub it in."

"That shit burns."

"No. That shit tingles. Rub it in, you will enjoy it, trust me."

"You won't."

She narrowed her eyes at him, not that he could see her annoyance. It was carefully hidden behind her periwinkle blue mask.

"Does it look like you will be touching me?" She bit out.

"No, Mistress," he said after a tense silence.

"Better. Now, me."

She had to suppress her moans of pleasure as Thomas massaged and rubbed oil over her body. Moisture pooled in her pussy as he ran his hands over her breasts and between her legs. But that moisture was for her alone, trapped inside a layer of vinyl. She contemplated having him rub her off, but that was not tonight's game.

"Enough," she said before she lost control of her resolve. "You, there." She pointed Thomas to a solid length of wood, like a column, with chains and manacles bolted to the sides. "Brace your hands."

Obediently, Thomas did as he was told. She reached around him, pressing against his body and she fasted his wrist chains to the block.

Mistress picked up another bottle of oil and poured it over herself. With one hand hooked through the collar at his neck, she ran her other hand down his back, sliding her hand between the firm muscular cheeks of his ass. His muscles tightened, temporarily stopping her hand. She tightened her hold on the collar, and with a heavy sigh, he relaxed. He let out a strangled gasp when her finger found the puckered entrance she so wanted to toy with.

She started with one finger, gliding it around and then pressing against the tight muscles. Resistance gave way and she slid her finger in. The compression was tight. She felt it in her pussy, even though she had every intention of denying herself that pleasure.

Thomas groaned out a "Yes, Mistress," without any prompting.

"Good boy," she purred as she slid a second finger into the tight cavity.

Thomas clenched and rocked his hips away from her. Before she could scold him, he was pressing back against her hand, eager for her to begin thrusting and fucking him.

"Slowly," she commanded.

Thomas made a pitiful moan. "Please, Mistress."

He had asked so nicely. She released her grip on his collar and reached around his hips. Her oiled-up breasts slid against his firm back. He let out another needful sound when she wrapped her fingers around his cock. It was longer and thicker now that it was happy and not recoiling from too much spicy lube.

Oh, Thomas liked a good prostate probing. Mistress began stroking his hard cock in time to thrusting her fingers deep into his ass. She undulated against his back as he rocked his hips back and forth. She thrust his fingers in his ass and stroked his cock.

Thomas lost his sense of rhythm. The muscles in his ass clenched almost painfully around her fingers. Abruptly she pulled her fingers free of his ass.

Thomas let out a strangled gurgle. She wasn't sure if it was disappointment in losing the fingers up his ass or the impending orgasm that elicited the sound. She turned him. Managed to the column he was forced to arch his back, thrusting his hips out to her. She put her hand back on his cock. She pumped delighted in the feel of his throbbing and pulsing cock. His eye clenched and he froze on a forward thrust.

His cum splashed forth like being shot from a fire hose.

Mistress giggled as she was showered in his jizz. "Don't stop," she commanded.

She continued to pump his cock and force him to cum as she danced under his shot.

He shuddered and fell back against the column.

"Done already?" A dribble of cum ran across the lens of her mask.

With the satisfaction of a hand job well done, Mistress pressed a small call button next to the door.

There was a knock and then the door opened. The woman dressed like a blue fairy from earlier stood with an armful of towels. "Do you require clean-up?"

"Oh, yes I do," Mistress purred as she pulled the other woman into her playroom.

Little Projects

G ladys stood in the middle of the street. Her afternoon wine
was disguised in a dark mug. To any casual observer, it
would appear that she was holding a hot cup— coffee or tea—
and chatting with her neighbors. That was the point.

The other ladies had various other libations. Gladys knew for
a fact that Ester had vodka in her water bottle. Mary probably
was the only one to actually have coffee in her coffee cup. She
always held it with two hands wrapped around and steam
coming from the open top. Even on hot summer days, Mary
looked cold.

"I don't know what Wilfred thinks he's doing. He knows I'll
call in another complaint if he's out there barbequing naked,"
Mary complained.

"He's trying hard to audition for you, Mary," Gladys cackled.

"It's anything but hard," Mary said with a roll of her eyes.

Bev did a spit take with her drink. "Good lord, warn a
person."

Gladys saw a cyclist turn the corner and head down Bluebird
Lane. He was definitely not from their neighborhood. Century
Lawn. The name sounded more like a cemetery than a
neighborhood. Mostly everyone, biding their time before being

buried, was exclusively of retirement age. This young man was not a local resident.

He swished past with a nod and what sounded like an "afternoon ladies," before heading away. Gladys turned to watch him cycle past.

All four ladies watched the cyclist as they continued their conversation.

"Speaking of hard," Ester sighed. "I miss a nice, firm young body. I'm tired of my options being Wilfred or that gigolo Hank."

"Hank thinks because he has a little blue pill he has the only functional penis in and two-mile radius"

"He does have the only functional penis—"

"Nonsense, I have a perfectly functional penis," Bev chimed in.

Everyone's attention turned back to her.

"It's battery-powered, and it does a perfectly fine job."

Everyone giggled.

"I'm tired of battery-operated, I want a real man," Gladys said with a sigh as she noticed the cyclist was back.

She felt a flutter in her chest, probably angina when he stopped next to their little group.

"Sorry to interrupt ladies, but I seem to be lost," he said.

Sweat glistened on firm square pectorals.

"Looks like you've lost your shirt," Mary said. "Aren't you cold?"

"No, ma'am. It's hot out here."

"What can we help you find?" Bev asked.

"I'm supposed to be doing some odd jobs on Bluebird Court, and, well everything right around here—" he twirled his hand in the air— "is all Bluebird, lane, avenue, circle, but I can't find court. And once I'm out of the Bluebirds, everything is Cardinal this Cardinal that."

"I think the person who named the streets had a vendetta against an older relative. Imagine how hard it is for people with memory issues," Gladys said. She let her eyes roam over the man in front of her. She sighed.

"So you do odd jobs? How much do you charge?" she asked.

"What's the project?" He asked with a smile.

Her nipples reacted in ways she had almost forgotten about. Neither Wilfred nor Hank could get that kind of a reaction from her. And Hank had tried.

"I'll break something," she said with a guttural purr.

"I can fix that," he chuckled.

"I'm pretty sure I have a kitchen full of broken projects," Bev announced.

"I do my best work in the kitchen."

"Oh, you cook?" Mary asked.

"I wouldn't call it cooking, more like, mixing it up."

"Bluebird Court is hidden off of Bluebird Circle," Mary said, oblivious to his cheeky meaning.

The man cut a charming smile to Mary and thanked her.

"I'm right here"—Gladys pointed to her house— "come by when you're finished. I'm sure I have a shirt for you."

He took a long hard look at her house before returning his gaze to her. "I'll be back in a couple of hours."

No one said anything as he rode off.

"Gladys, did you just do what I think you did?" Ester asked.

"I'll let you know tomorrow."

"Oh no, I'm going to be there," Ester said firmly.

"You're going to watch him work?" Mary asked.

Gladys shook her head, poor clueless Mary. "No, hun. She's gonna help him."

Two hours and twenty-five minutes later...

Nerves danced in Gladys's stomach when she heard the doorbell. She stood and crossed her living room, finishing another glass of wine as she did. She opened the door and let out a ragged breath. Shirtless, sweaty, and all man, the cyclist leaned against the door frame.

"So, you have a job for me?"

"What's your name, hun?" Gladys asked as she stepped back letting him step inside.

She brushed against him as she closed the door.

"Mike," he said.

"Mike. That's a good strong name. I need some assistance with something in my bedroom that needs pounding."

"Pounding?"

"Yeah, there's a couple of things that need a good banging."

"I'm particularly good at banging." His eyes narrowed as he scanned her bathrobe. "Lead the way."

Gladys remembered how to sway her hips somewhere between the front door and her bedroom door. And then she remembered that this was less of seduction and more a direct transaction. She dropped her robe and opened her bedroom door.

Mike stepped through. Gladys closed the door as she stepped in behind.

Ester smiled back from the bed, a sheet draped across her breasts.

Mike looked from one to the other of the women. He nodded his head as he swung his backpack onto the floor and kicked off his shoes.

"Ladies," he said as he undid his belt. "I typically charge hourly and not by the project. And I pride myself on complete job satisfaction."

They both let out low appreciative moans when Mike dropped his shorts, and a long girthy cock emerged.

"Your fee is on the dresser," Ester said pointing to the dresser behind him.

He wrapped a hand around his base. "I could use some encouragement it seems."

He stepped over to the bed and climbed in.

Gladys pushed him onto his back and leaned into his lap. She took his long length onto her mouth. He was musk and salt, and she had forgotten how good a man could taste.

Ester squealed, and a quick glance let Gladys know that Mike had found a use for his hands and mouth.

A few licks were all Mike needed to be primed. Gladys released him. She looked up to see Ester's eyes rolling back into her head as she sat on his face.

"Oh, fuck. So good, so good," Ester whined. Before long, she sounded like a squirrel. She had her hands clamped on her breasts and she rode his face like some grocery store quarter-a-ride mechanical pony.

Ester convulsed, and for a moment Gladys was concerned they had pushed her friend too far. But then she sagged with a satisfied sigh and fell to the side. "I haven't had an orgasm like that in years."

Mike, grinning ear to ear, wiped his face and looked at Gladys. "Didn't you say there was something that needed banging?"

"Oh, yeah." Gladys lay back and let her knees drop to the side.

"Don't be too rough, she's had a hip replacement," Ester said in a sleepy voice.

Mike positioned himself above Gladys. He raised his eyebrows in question.

"Break me," she said, handing up a bottle of lube.

"Yes, ma'am," was all he said. He squeezed lube over her exposed pussy, and into his hand before rubbing it over his cock. Unceremoniously he drove his cock into her cunt.

She screamed and beat her fists against the mattress. She hadn't had anything big and that hard between her legs in decades. He stretched her out. She was going to be floppy for days after this.

His dick pounded into her. She started seeing stars from the beginning as he pumped life back into her.

Once the initial shock wore off, Gladys remembered how to fuck back and lifted his hips to thrust against Mike.

They were grunting and thrusting. This wasn't sex, it was a mission they both took very seriously. She wanted to get off, and he was going to get her there.

He arched his back and found her breasts with his mouth. Sucking on her nipple was a direct connection to her clit. It was what she needed to begin her crash over the cliff of orgasm. Her muscles began gathering their power with a rhythmic sucking action. Soon she had no control and the muscle spasms reverberated through her body. She remembered this feeling. Hank did not know how to create this effect. No one had for a long time.

With one final clamping muscle spasm, Gladys felt like she had a grip so firm around Mike's cock inside of her, that she was going to rip the glorious member off his body.

And then she felt it, the warmth spreading as he reached his pinnacle and spurted into her.

She lay wasted, limp, unable to move any muscles.

Mike rolled out of bed and was pulling his shorts on. Ester snored, knocked out.

"You should be able to find a shirt in there," Gladys pointed to her closet.

"You think you'll have any more little projects for me?" he asked, pulling on a t-shirt.

"I'm sure I will, why don't you swing by tomorrow.

Special Delivery

The doorbell rang. Nancy wrapped her robe around her a little more securely, blew her nose, and opened the door.

"You order a six-inch smoked turkey?"

The young man at the door was one of those slick guys, tight fade with extra length on top. The kind of guy that Nancy always looked twice at. She liked her men tough and on the prettier side — maybe a little overcompensating on the attitude because genetics landed them with more refined features. This guy was dressed immaculately, even if wearing sports-themed gear. Shoes pristine white, no creases, same with the hat. He was hot.

His eyes were ridiculously large, and his jawline…

His jawline was a little too soft, his neck perfectly slender, and…oh wow, no Adam's apple. He wasn't a pretty little boy, no, she was a masculine-presenting woman.

The delivery woman eyed Nancy up and down.

Nancy gulped and tried not to blush. All thoughts of being miserable gone with a little positive attention.

"You okay, baby?" she asked.

Nancy gave a weak nod. "I'm okay, been better but, I'll survive." She reached out for the bag with her sandwich. "This will help."

"Seems to me six inches isn't going to help you at all," the delivery hottie said.

Nancy scoffed. "Six inches is all I'm willing to take. Eight inches is what got me messed up."

The sexy little smirk dropped from the hottie's face. "Did some guy hurt you? I can mess him up for you."

"Oh my god, that's so sweet. No. Well, yes, he broke my heart, but nothing physical."

"I got what you need to get over your heartache."

Nancy, trying not to giggle at the obvious flirting, shook the bag with the food. "You got something better than six inches? I mean twelve is just so excessive, and stuffing that much in me just ends up hurting."

The sexy smirk was back, accompanied by a lower lip bite. Gleaming white teeth against the dark pink of her lips, and Nancy's nipples peaked to attention. A throbbing of lust began to pulse at her core. This woman's flirt game was strong. Nancy was already wet and What's-his-name was fast becoming a memory.

Nancy lowered her eyes with a tilt of her head and looked back at the other woman through her eyelashes. She licked her lips.

"What time do you," she swallowed— not quite believing she was doing this— "get off."

She heaved a big sigh, pushing her boobs out. They were hidden under a thick layer of a plush robe.

"Tell you what"— the hottie trailed her fingers over her chin, framing her lower face— "my shift ends in a couple of hours. Why don't I swing by and see how you liked that sandwich. Customer satisfaction and all that is important at our shop."

Nancy nodded, words had escaped her. She had never propositioned a delivery person before, and certainly not a woman.

"I'll see you later, baby."

"Wait." Nancy stepped out the door as the other woman walked away. "What's your name? I'm Nancy."

"Nice to meet you, Nancy. Melinda, call me Mel."

Nancy smiled like a fool and stepped back into her apartment.

Two hours later…

Nancy sat curled up on her couch watching TV when the doorbell rang. She wrapped her robe a little more securely around her and fluffed her hair.

"Hey. Baby." Mel stood on the other side of the door. She had changed, no longer in tough-guy athletics, she now wore a slim-fitting suit.

Nancy had a hard time breathing. Mel was stunning. Sexy in a spy movie kind of way. She had showered and changed and all Nancy had managed was to put on some make-up.

She stepped back, gesturing for Mel to come in.

"I wasn't sure what you were into, so I brought some toys. If six inches isn't enough, eight is all wrong, and twelve too much, I have a ten incher in here that might just be perfect for you." Mel stepped in and swung a duffle bag from her shoulder.

Nancy was stunned. No one had ever come prepared before. Then again What's-his-name thought he was the end all be all of sex machines.

"What if I don't know what I like?" Nancy asked.

Mel reached out and tugged at the belt of Nancy's robe. It fell open. There was nothing but skin underneath.

"I think you know exactly what you want," Mel said as she stepped in closer and reached a hand into the robe. She found Nancy's breast with its peaked nipple.

Nancy's nipple squeezed as if it was reaching out for Mel's palm before it was engulfed in soft warmth.

Nancy gasped. Mel's hand was incredibly soft.

Mel cupped, and then pressed more firmly, and then pinched Nancy's nipple.

It hurt in the best way possible, and Nancy moaned. Before she knew it Mel's mouth was on hers, stealing her sound, and encouraging others.

If Nancy had thought Mel's hands were soft, she was lost against the softness of her mouth. Mel's kisses were firm and giving, yet they took as well. Her teeth were not too sharp, and she never bit very hard, but she bit, and it was thrilling.

She continued to knead Nancy's breast. Her other hand slipped around her back and pulled Nancy against her, torso to torso.

Nancy didn't know what to do with her hands. She ran them over Mel's clothed form, before realizing she could at least take her own off. She let the robe slip off her shoulders. Mel deepened their kiss, and Nancy lost herself to the feel of the other woman.

She had been all nervous waiting for Mel to arrive at the end of her shift. Nerves had danced in anticipation and in terror.

"I don't know what to do with another woman," she blurted out her confession.

"Do you know what your body likes?" Mel's voice was a soothing purr. She shrugged out of the suit coat and began unbuttoning the vest she wore over the crisply pressed shirt. Her hand trailed over Nancy's exposed skin.

Nancy nodded mutely.

Mel chuckled. "We have the same parts. Just do what you like to be done to you."

"Ah…" Nancy hesitated. "I like dick."

Mel smirked. The expression made Nancy weak in the knees and even wetter between her legs. "I have a selection in the bag. Why don't you show me your bedroom."

Nancy nodded and took Mel's hand, hesitating only long enough for the other woman to pick up her bag of goodies. She led Mel down the short hall and into her room. Her preparations for this evening not only included taking her clothes off but also putting clean sheets on the bed.

Mel didn't waste any time, pulling the rest of her clothes off. Her breasts were small and perky, unlike Nancy's more ample figure.

Nancy sat in the middle of her bed, nerves building, ready to explode. When Mel crawled to her, she could barely restrain herself from pulling Mel to her.

They fell back in a tangle of limbs. Nancy giggled as a soft breast brushed against her own. It was an utterly unexpected sensation. She pulled back from Mel's kisses grabbed her own boob and directed her nipple to touch and cross against Mel's. It tickled.

Mel cupped her breast and held it up for Nancy. She lowered her head and licked. When Mel shuddered, Nancy grew bolder and sucked the offered nipple in with enthusiasm. Her other hand-kneaded and massaged the other breast.

The nipple under Nancy's tongue was sweet and long. She enjoyed the noises she could coax from the other woman, simply by sucking and biting. Easy access to the nipples without a mouthful of chest hair was a bonus.

Mel grabbed the hand on her boob and dragged it down her body, directing Nancy's fingers to the space between her legs.

Nancy remembered what Mel had said, just do what you like. What Nancy liked were a little tingle and well-oiled fingers. She pulled away from Mel and crawled over the other woman's body to rummage through her bedside table drawer. She made a noise indicating success and held the bottle of massage oil up so Mel could see it.

"Oh, I approve."

"It's a little tingly. You said to do what I like. I like this."

Mel held her hand, palm up, and ran it down her body as if she were offering up what was on display. "I'm yours to explore. If you like it, I'm sure I will too."

Nancy poured the oil into her hand, and then directly onto Mel's pussy. It was cute and tight, her clit poked out like a little tongue sticking out. She had a crop of well-groomed pubes, a tight faded top and bottom.

She closed her eyes and let her fingers slide over the lips between Mel's legs. The skin was soft and slick with the oil.

Mel moaned and thrust her hips up to meet Nancy's fingers. Nancy spread Mel's pussy and let her finger trail through the folds. Mel's eyes were closed and her head tossed back. She looked like she was enjoying the feeling.

Nancy lowered her mouth to the closet pert nipple and sucked. It took her a long moment to find the right rhythm of fingering and sucking. She focused on Mel's clit, circle, circle, drip back and in, and back to circling the clit.

Nancy didn't realize how amazing it would be to finger fuck another woman. Giving head wasn't the same. Men always grabbed her head and tried to control the action, but Mel wasn't. She had given herself over to Nancy's exploration.

Nancy took a deep breath and before she could change her mind, she dropped the nipple in her mouth and placed her first kiss against a pussy.

Mel's legs spread even wider, and her hips pressed up against Nancy's face. Mel tasted of the spicy oil, and something much more primal. Sex, she tasted of sex, orgasms, and fucking.

Nancy's tongue went everywhere, deep into Mel's hole, and then wrapped around her clit. Nancy now understood the fascination with eating out a pussy. She decided she was able to step up to the next level, fingers in. Really in, not a teasing dip, but thrust deep. Pumping fucking action.

Mel's body sucked at her fingers. The sensation was new, not unexpected, but surprising nonetheless.

Mel's orgasm on her face and on her fingers was ambrosia, an aphrodisiac. Nancy lapped up Mel's honey and laughed as her fingers were grabbed and squeezed in a frenzy.

"Damn, you sure you didn't know what you were doing?" Mel asked after a moment of limp panting.

Nancy shook her head.

"Well brace yourself, baby. It's my turn." Mel leaned over the side of the bed and held up a large blue dildo.

The Application

R ed pouty lips, open and glistening with need, were perfectly framed with crisp black hairs. Silken tawny thighs bound in leather straps and chains flanked the perfect photo of the perfect pussy. It was hot, used, and ready for more.

Another man's cum dripped from the hole, teasing that it wasn't him who had made that mess or fucked that woman.

Robert shifted in his chair. He was too old to get a raging hard-on from the average spank bank cream-pie image. But nothing about the photo on his phone was average.

He looked up when he heard a knock on his office door.

"Come in," he called out.

Sophi Rodriguez stepped through the door. She had a cloud of black hair and was wrapped in a red dress that on any other woman would be office appropriate. On Sophi, it was practically indecent.

Robert gestured for her to have a seat. She crossed his office with a walk that would raise wood in the dead. If women walked to the beat of a drummer, Robert would say the average woman walked to a high school marching band. Standard, step step step. Maybe a flourish of a wiggle every now and again. When Sophi walked, there had to be a sweaty band banging out a rumba rhythm somewhere.

"You wanted to see me?" she asked nervously. Was her lower lip quivering?

"We have a potential problem. As I see it this could go several ways. It all depends on how you want to deal with it."

He slid his phone across his desk, screen side down.

Sophi picked up the phone, nodded, and placed it back on the desk. "I see."

"Care to share how that image made it to my phone? Was it an embarrassing accident that I should delete and forget about ever seeing?"

"I hope not. I sent it."

He sat up a little straighter in his chair and cleared his throat. "You sent it? Do you realize how many HR violations you have made by sending this to my phone?"

She blinked her large dark eyes at him. Robert couldn't help but compare the red lips on her face to the red lips he knew were between her legs. He wanted to get his mouth on both of them.

"I thought I was applying for a job," she said, her voice low and trembling.

"What job exactly did you think you were applying for?"

She stood, smoothed her dress over her hips, and took a few steps across the office, closing the door.

Robert heard the distinct click of the lock. She stepped to the side and twisted the blinds closed. She turned and leaned against the door frame, trailed her finger up and down the deep V-neck of her dress, slipping it open more.

Her hips moved and he swore he could hear the voom vava voom bump and grind of a lounge band in her movements. She walked around to his side of the desk and perched her ass on his desk.

"This one," she said as she opened the slit of her dress exposing warm thick thighs and a bright red matching thong.

"Did I do wrong? You should punish me."

She rolled her hips toward him, sweeping the skirt of her dress up as she positioned herself. Her round ample ass was exposed as she leaned over his desk.

Robert was too old to cream himself, but fuck if he wasn't close.

"Are you going to spank me, daddy?"

She blinked those big eyes at him. Robert could not believe his luck. He had no intentions of turning her into HR, and no plans of deleting her dripping wet cunt from his phone. He had wanted to see if she would blush, deny everything, squirm. But this unexpected turn was so much better.

He stood, rolling his chair back. He leaned over her, his hand grabbing onto her full ass.

"You're right, you should be punished for distracting me that way." He slapped his hand against her skin.

Sophi let out more of an appreciative "ah" than a moan as his hand made contact. The smack was louder than Robert expected. He laced his fingers into her hair and drew her head back with a fist full of her hair.

"Stay right there," he commanded.

He righted himself and crossed the office. On the bookshelf next to the door was a white noise machine and a stereo. They were specifically meant to mask private conversations and keep corporate secrets inside his office.

With music now filling the office, he returned to Sophi's side.

He ran a single finger up the crease of her pussy, feeling her through the thin fabric of the thong. This time she gasped.

He rubbed his hand in a circle over the spot where ass gave way to taint. He smacked her hard enough to leave a red handprint on her flesh.

"How bad have you been?"

"I've been very bad. I could be badder for you."

Her voice trailed promises of spicy heat down his spine and wrapped a vice around his balls. She might be able to take more spanks, but he didn't know if he could. His need to spank that skin with something other than his hand was quickly becoming painful.

He hit her again, and she moaned. It was more pleasure than pain for her.

He half wished she had worn the leather garters so he could move her around. Instead, he spread her cheeks and looked at her puckered hole. He licked his finger and sank it knuckle deep.

Sophi jumped, collapsing across his desk with a yelp.

He began fucking her ass. "How bad have you been?"

Sophi struggled to speak. "This bad, oh definitely this bad." She pressed her hips back and sank a little deeper onto his finger.

With one finger in, he smacked her with his other hand. Sophie responded with a guttural moan and a rocking of her hips. With each smack and each thrust, Sophi thrust back as if she wanted more.

He removed his finger and crossed the office. He pulled several tissues from a box and pumped hand sanitizer onto his hand. He wiped his finger and hand clean. Clean enough for now.

Sophi's tan ass was splotched with pink. Some areas more angry red than others.

Robert unfastened his belt and zipper. He pushed his pants down his thighs. His cock was hard and dripping with pre-cum. He was more than ready. He pulled the red thong to the side and took in Sophi's dripping wet pussy, exposed to him in person for the first time. It was more impressive than the photo, and that was one fucking good photograph.

Fingers bit into the flesh on the side of her hips as Robert thrust his eager cock home. She bounced against the desk as he fucked her with hard, almost angry thrusts.

"Fuck," he grunted. She felt too good, all wet hot with grabbing sucking muscles.

"Fuck," he yelled as his entire being seized up. Reality turned inside out as his balls squeezed hard against his body and cum pulsed out of him with the pressure of a fire hose.

He sat back in his desk chair with a thump.

"Show me," he demanded.

Sophi pushed off the desk and turned, again perching her ass on the edge of his desk. She reached forward, wrapped her hand around his tie, and pulled him closer. Once she had him where she wanted him, she placed one foot on either side, dropping her knees to the side, exposing her rode-hard pussy, dripping with his cum.

Robert shuddered, his body trying to produce more jizz to spray, but incapable.

He wrapped his large hands over her thighs and lowered his head so that his lips finally were on hers.

This time Sophi squealed and bucked against his face until she was too limp to move.

Robert wiped his mouth as he sat back. A satisfied grin crossed his face.

"So," Sophi panted, "did I get the job?"

In the Stacks

♥

G raham tried not to watch the ass in front of him. It went
Boom-Boom-Boom with hips that jiggled with every step.
Other butts didn't move so violently when just walking. This one
did. It reminded him of a line from a movie once, something
about two cats fighting in a bag. It was meant as a compliment.

The woman to whom the ass belonged terrified him. He didn't
think she would appreciate being told her backside not only
inspired an erection so hard he was having difficulty walking,
but her hips were conducting their own strategic ground
maneuvers. He was fairly certain by the time they got to where
they were going, his trousers were going to be collateral damage.

Each sway, each clench of muscle as her weight shifted sent
another electrified pulse straight through his balls. He could
barely breathe. And to think, today of all days, he didn't have his
rescue inhaler with him.

Sweat caused his glasses to slide down his nose. He shrugged
his shoulder against his face, trying to reposition the corrective
eyewear. His arms were full of books.

Every few moments the woman, he no longer thought of her
as the librarian, he couldn't. Librarians were mousey meek
things, gentle souls in cardigans. This woman was sex on legs.

She was a man-eater with a reputation of busting the balls of anyone who misbehaved in her domain. But like the stereotype in his head, she was crazy smart. She knew every research journal, every commercial magazine, every inch of microfiche, every web portal, every book ever printed. She was a walking library.

Part of Graham had always thought that was the sexiest thing about her. She didn't have the answers, she knew where to find the answers.

He took in a shuddering breath, just thinking about how she knew how to find what he needed. She always stayed behind her reference desk scribbling catalog numbers on scraps of paper and sending him on his way. But not today. Today she was personally escorting him to the stacks, a graduate student's combined research dream and nightmare.

Her heels clicked a rhythm that her ass responded to in a wet dream dance number. Graham had already forgotten more than once what he was doing here. Every few moments she would stop and he would stare dumbfoundedly as she placed another tome into his arms. She would smile, her dark eyes would sparkle, and he would lose more brain cells as blood flow to his brain diminished again.

The collection was growing, and he had to strain his neck to look over the stack in his arms to appreciate the view. She had thick dark hair midway down her back, not worn up in a messy bun, but left down in a cascade of loops and curls like a Hollywood starlet. The dress she wore hid precisely nothing about her figure, from her buxom proportions to her wasp waist to that ass that would provide the visions for his jacking off from now until forever. He hoped visions of that ass would give him pleasure long into his old age.

Graham about dropped the books in his arms when suddenly she stopped and twirled around. Her eyes were narrowed, and that gleam looked dangerous.

"You've been staring awfully hard at my ass," she accused.

He struggled to swallow around the boulder that suddenly appeared in his throat. Busted.

She raked her gaze down to his toes before returning to meet his eyes.

"That, really?" She darted her eyes back down.

He felt the look like laser beams when she stopped at the obvious bulge in his pants. With his arms full of research he had no way to adjust or hide his obvious arousal.

"Um…" was all he could manage to articulate.

"What do you take me for? Some object for your pleasure?"

"Na, na, na… no," he managed to stammer.

She stepped closer and Graham backed away, crashing into the shelf of books.

"What do you plan on doing about it?" She practically snarled.

He clutched the books tight to his chest as if they could protect him. She had seen his hard-on, there was no denying it. He was caught, trapped. His inner thoughts were betrayed by his physical reaction.

"Sa, sa… sorry. I'm trying to ignore it, hoping it goes away. It's not exactly a voluntary response."

She stepped closer.

Graham scooted along the shelf, pressing his back into the cool metal in a failed attempt to escape her onslaught. He groaned as his balls tightened and pulled hard to his body. He should have been flaccid with fear, but no, he was harder than ever. More turned on in his terror than he should ever have been.

He yelped when her hand cupped his crotch. His hips didn't retreat as they should have, they pressed forward into the warmth of her hand.

She stroked him through his clothes. He dropped his armload of books. Scattering all of his future reading on the floor. He waited for her to chastise him, instead she unzipped his pants.

Graham shoved a balled-up fist into his mouth to stop him from yelling. With his other hand, he held onto a shelf behind him for dear life. He didn't know if he was going to survive this. He didn't necessarily care.

She grabbed a little hard. "You would want me to take care of this wouldn't you?"

Graham managed to nod. Of course, he wanted her, that's what the throbbing erection was all about. Somehow he had enough muscle control to slowly nod his head.

She smiled, but it wasn't a friendly grin. It had sharp teeth and reminded him of a shark.

He closed his eyes. He was going to die, and he didn't feel like witnessing it. He hissed in at the sensation as he felt air on his ass, and his cock was no longer confined by his clothes.

He wanted to cry when he felt the first lick of her wet tongue along the thick vein on the underside of his cock. Teeth scraped the edges of his dick, and everything in his body pulsed and jumped.

Lips that he knew were lush and thick wrapped around his head and a sudden sucking pressure tried to pull his soul out through his dick. He wanted to fold in on himself and let her drag him through the singularity of a straw.

He was vaguely aware of his location, but all of that extraneous information no longer mattered. All there was in all of existence at that moment was her warm wet mouth taking in his cock, inch by agonizingly slow inch. Each time she seemed to consume more of him, her lips would slide back and she would tease with a combination of a gentle scraping of teeth and a swirling flick of the tongue over his tip.

He didn't understand how he could still be standing, still have an erection that was trying to reach out to her. One of her hands circled his base and cupped his balls. The other dug nails into his ass. Her breasts pressed against his knees. He wanted to reach down and thread his fingers into her hair, feel the softness, rub it against his skin.

Every time he started to let go of the self, he felt like he was falling, going to collapse into the void. His grasp of the shelf was the only thing keeping him connected to reality.

Her breath caressed him, her mouth consumed him. There were no more thoughts in his head, only sensation. The slide of warmth combined with cool air had his hips pressing forward, seeking the warmth again.

Each time there was more warmth, more mouth, more sucking pull. Her tongue danced around his shaft. Soft breasts rubbed against his legs. Nails bit as she now had both ass cheeks in her hands, and she was pulling them apart, exposing his butt hole to the cool air of the climate-controlled stacks.

He had no control of his body. All actions, all movements were for the single need of her mouth, her throat to hold him, to stroke his length, to suck him in. His hips rocked, and she hummed.

He froze. She hadn't made any sounds that he had been aware of up until that point. He repeated the movement, and she hummed again. Her lips vibrated along his length.

Holy fuck, that felt good!

She continued to hum, and he continued to fuck her mouth. He finally let go of the shelf and fisted her hair, holding her head close to him. He moved, and she pulled him to her. Her mouth was in control, but he wanted to participate, the movement of his hips was involuntary. He couldn't stop them at this point even if he wanted.

His balls squeezed hard, and the sudden rush of cum up through his system and out his cock took everything from him. He seized up, no muscles able to function as his body was capable of a single function, and that was to shoot his load.

The librarian laughed and hummed and sucked. She pulled everything Grahm could produce from him. When he felt as if there wasn't anymore in him, she continued to suck him in. She finally relented, releasing his ass with a drag of her nails over his flesh. As wiped the corners of her mouth with a single finger, and licked her lips.

She handed him one of the previously dropped books as she stood.

"Now, where were we?" she asked, turning and stepping away from that particular area of shelving.

Graham scrambled to pull up his pants, picked up all the books, and followed after her.

The Birthday Present

<hr />

"You want me to do what?" She wasn't shrieking, but her voice was shrill, and the pitch was winding higher. "You just want to fuck another woman. I know what's really going on here."

"Babe, babe, no. That's not it at all, I swear," he lied. He did want to fuck another woman, but at the same time he was fucking his wife.

He had proposed as a little birthday present they could have a threesome. Get a little wild. He wanted an excuse to openly fuck his girlfriend. If the wife agreed to incorporate his side piece, he wouldn't feel so guilty. After all, anything after their little ménage a trois, he could claim as 'but I thought it would be okay."

"Honey, you're always saying how you never had a chance to be wild and crazy. Now I'm saying let's be wild and crazy. If you want to try a sex club, let's go to a sex club—"

"I don't want to go to a sex club," she said with a heavy sigh.

"But you have said you always wondered what it would be like to have a three-way."

She glared up at him through her lashes. He knew that look. She was close to giving in.

"Okay, so how does one go about finding a third?"

"Let me take care of that. There are dating apps online."

"I want to meet her first," she demanded.

"of course, of course."

That was two weeks ago. Now they sat at a table waiting for their potential third to arrive.

His wife was visibly nervous. He had a hard time hiding the shit-eating grin on his face. The wife was about to meet the girlfriend and didn't have a clue. The girlfriend knew and she was in on the scam.

"Nice to see you again Greg," a beautiful young woman said.

"Delilah," he nodded.

She reached out, and when his wife slid her fingers into Delilah's hand, she kissed the other woman's knuckles. Her eyes never broke contact with his wife's. MaryJean was going to say yes, he could see it in the way she responded to Delilah.

"Please join us," MaryJean said.

"That is the plan, isn't it?" Delilah slid into the chair next to MaryJean and leaned into her personal space.

Greg was pleased they were getting along so well.

After his birthday dinner, and indulging in cake at the restaurant, Delilah drove MaryJean in her car, while he followed behind. MaryJean was the one to invite Delilah over for a nightcap, and see what developed. He wanted to rub his hands together in wicked glee. Instead, he rubbed his dick, priming the pump for action soon to come.

When he got home, they were already inside. He followed the sound of giggles to find them with glasses of wine and half undressed in the bedroom. They were getting things started.

"Alright!" he said. He kicked off his shoes and began stripping off his clothes.

MaryJean glanced over her shoulder at him before returning her attention to Delilah.

Her shirt was off and her tits were out. MaryJean's eyes rolled up into her head and she bit her lip as Delilah played with her nipples.

Greg sidled up behind Delilah, who was also shirtless, wearing just a pair of red panties. He wrapped his hands around her and cupped her breasts. She elbowed him in the ribs.

"Did you ask?" she sneered at him.

"What?" he was confused.

"Excuse me," she said to MaryJean. She turned around to face Greg who hadn't bothered to fully remove his pants and stood in front of her without a shirt on and his pants pushed down his thighs. She glared at his cock.

Greg felt it deflate against her judgment.

"You don't get to come in here and feel me up without asking permission. Now, take your clothes off and stand over there"— she pointed over to the closet— "and learn something."

Greg kicked out of his pants and stomped over to the corner like he was put on a time-out and was pouting.

Delilah returned her attention to MaryJean. She reached out and caressed the sides of his wife's boobs. MaryJean shuddered and sighed.

"Now, do that to me." Delilah picked up MaryJean's hands and placed them on her ribs.

She leaned in as MaryJean followed orders.

"I never knew breasts were so fascinating," MaryJean said with a giggle.

"If you think boobs are fun, just wait." Delilah took MaryJean's hand and put it in her panties.

Greg gulped. He never thought watching his wife touch another woman would be so fucking hot. He wrapped his hand around his cock, and began stroking.

"Are you ready for more advanced fun?" Delilah asked as she pushed her panties down.

MaryJean made a disappointed noise as her plaything was removed from her reach.

Greg had never imagined when she had said she wanted a ménage with him and his wife, that she would be so well versed in how to orchestrate their actions. His wife had never touched or even kissed another girl. And now she was fingering Delilah with enthusiasm.

Delilah pushed MaryJean onto her back and crawled up her body. Their breasts brushed together.

Greg groaned and pumped his hand harder.

MaryJean moaned as Delilah kissed her. Their tongues danced, as they savored each other's mouths. Greg wanted to be in the middle of that sandwich. He was feeling left out, standing all alone in the corner with just his hand as company.

"Hey, it's my turn," he demanded, finally stepping up to the bed.

"Wait," demanded Delilah. "It's MaryJean's turn."

She shoved him back. He stretched out along the top edge of the bed, casting pillows aside to make himself more comfortable.

Delilah broke away from MaryJean who lay back on the bed. She crawled and lifted until she could press a nipple into MaryJean's mouth.

Greg moaned. It was so hot.

Delilah looked up at him. "Finish taking her clothes off," she tilted her head at his wife's legs.

Greg moved as told. He exposed MaryJean's wet pussy. His cock throbbed, balls tightening. He was ready to insert himself into this little combination.

Delilah removed her boob from MaryJean's mouth and continued to climb up her body until her sex was positioned directly over MaryJean's face.

"Kiss me," she told the other woman.

"What, I don't know how to do that," MaryJean sounded panicked.

"Yes you do. You know how to kiss. Now kiss me."

MaryJean closed her eyes and wrapping her arms around Delilah's hips, slanted her mouth over the other woman's pussy.

Delilah moaned. "Now Greg, now."

Eager to join the party Greg went for the closest hole, his wife's soaking wetness. He grabbed her knees and spread her legs wide. His cock was already dripping, desperate to be thrust into heat and wetness. MaryJean managed to cry out even while she continued to feast between Delilah's legs.

He reached forward and grabbed Delilah's breasts, pulling her back against his chest. They rocked and fucked.

Greg lost his balance and fell to the side. He pulled Delilah off MaryJean's face.

"Hey!" she complained.

"Change of position," Delilah called out.

"Greg, down. MaryJean, you want dick or tongue?"

Greg lay on his back.

"Tongue," MaryJean answered.

Delilah threw her leg over Greg's hips and sank down on his cock. She held her hands out to MaryJean.

His view was blocked as MaryJean lowered against his face. He wrapped his hands over her hips and began thrusting his tongue into her depths as Delilah treated his dick like a stripper pole.

What he couldn't see was MaryJean and Delilah shoving their tongues down each other's throats and grabbing nipples.

He was covered in pussy, it was the best birthday present ever.

Alien Invasion

The neon lights flickered in a most ominous way.

"Can you see if the vacancy sign is working? It can't seem to decide if they have rooms or not."

"I don't want to. This is a murder motel. Look at it. We're in the middle of nowhere, it's a row of cinder block bunkers, and the only cars in the parking lot are broken down."

"I'm tired. I don't give a fuck. If you want anything resembling a bed and a bathroom, this is it. I don't know if you noticed or not, but there haven't been any hotels for miles, and who knows how long before we find anything."

With a grumble, Jake got out of the car. The lobby lights flickered and buzzed. Not seeing anyone, he smacked the 'ring for service' bell and began counting under his breath.

"Be right there!" the world's scratchiest voice, full of drinking too much and smoking for too many years, called out from somewhere behind the desk.

"Damn." He really didn't want to stay at the murder motel.

A human that matched the voice appeared, wrinkled, old, bald, in a stained undershirt with an unbuttoned flannel over it.

"Your lights are all fucked up, man. Can't tell if you have any vacancies or not."

The clerk looked around as if noticing the lights for the first time. "Martha! Tell room six to knock off the power play, they are going to blow a fuse!"

He turned his attention to Jake. "Yeah, we got rooms."

"Cool, cool. Let me just double-check with my cousin." Jake pushed out of the office. His skin crawled, and he wanted nothing more than to get the fuck out of there.

He opened the car door. "They have rooms, but I'm not staying. Let's go!"

His cousin popped a pill into his mouth and threw his head back, draining a can of soda,

"What the fuck was that?" Jake yelled.

"Sleeping pill. I told you I need to sleep."

"This place is creepy, and now you're going to snore," Jake whined.

"Get your own room. I'm done. Suck it up."

With a resigned sigh, Jake returned to the office. The clerk was waiting.

"I need two rooms," Jake said, holding up the same amount of fingers.

"You want themed or normal?"

Jake blinked at the question. "What kind of themes?"

"We got outer space, alien invasion, under the sea, we got hell," the man said with a shrug.

"Put my cousin in a normal room, I'll take alien invasion. Sounds like a laugh."

"You want turn-down service?"

"Why the fuck not?" It had to be good for a laugh, right?

He was handed two keys, actual keys. The tan key fob was for the regular room. The green fob for his themed room.

His cousin parked in front of the first room, making Jake lug his heavy bag to the far end of the motel and his themed room. He figured if he was going to get murdered he might as well be entertained.

"Fuck me. What is this Children of the Corn shit?"

The cinderblock walls of his room were painted with a mural of a cornfield. The bedspread was a design of concentric circles. A lamp shaped like a cartoon flying saucer hung in the middle of the ceiling. One of its lights was out. Behind the unit that held the TV, plywood cut out of a black and white cow added to the what the fuckery interior design.

The bathroom was blessedly plain, with white tiles with expected rust stains. The towels were thin and smelled vaguely of bleach, but they were clean. Jake shrugged out of his clothes and stepped into the shower, cranking the water too hot.

He scrubbed away the dust of the day's road trip with a tiny motel soap. Wrapping the biggest towel they had around his hips he stepped back into the room and turned the TV on. The cable selection was meager. He had clicked it over to the weather channel when there was a knock on his door.

Did murders knock?

Without thinking, Jake pulled the door wide. He had zero self-preservation when it came to welcoming his murderer in. Only she was an alien, big glowing green eyes, oval head, silver skin. Clearly, it was a mask, but it covered her entire head. After the second it took Jake to realize it was a mask, he checked out the rest of her costume, or rather body paint. Her skin was entirely silver, as was the tiny bikini that barely covered enough to keep her from being completely naked.

"Damn, they go all out on this theme," he said. He stumbled back giving his alien invader room to enter. His cousin was missing out.

"I see you're ready," she purred with an odd modulation. It must have been the mask distorting her voice.

Jake glanced down at his hips. The towel wasn't doing much at hiding his growing erection.

"You expected this?" he asked.

"Didn't you?" the sexy alien retorted as she snapped on plastic gloves she pulled from the drawers by the TV.

Jake watched wide-eyed as she filled her palms with lube and rubbed her hands together.

"Oh, hell yeah." He dropped the towel and lounged on the bed.

Her hands and lube were cold, and Jake jumped a bit when she wrapped them around his growing cock.

"If I knew what a turn-down service really was... I'm signing up for this every time." He tucked his hands behind his head and let her work his dick with slick strokes. He hissed when she cupped his balls. She cooed platitudes of endearment, praising his long thick cock, and outstanding ball.

She really knew what she was doing.

"You gonna take that mask off?"

The large mask wobbled as she shook her head. She did however release his balls and shoved her boobs in his face. He discovered he couldn't move his arms when he tried to reach out and touch her.

"What the fuck?" He was handcuffed to a bolt in the wall. Where the fuck had the cuffs been hidden?

The sexy alien ran her hands down his sides and pulled on his cock. He forgot to be upset. With one hand working his balls, she reached under him and grabbed his ass.

Before Jake knew what was happening she had flipped him over. With a few direct pushes against the backs of his legs, she had him on his knees.

When she pressed against his butt hole, his hips surged forward into her other hand. He was helpless when she pushed all the way into his ass.

"Oh, fuck," was all he managed. Thoughts of actually being murdered evaporated as one hand pumped his cock, and the other thrust against his prostate. His entire body was overcome with charged need, and he clenched everything. He yelled as if he really was being murdered when he shot his load.

Without the hot alien holding him up by his cock, he didn't have the energy to support himself and he sagged against the bed. He didn't even worry about still being chained to the wall when the alien girl patted him on the ass and left.

When he woke, he was in a normal-looking room, in his shorts under the covers. All vestiges of alien-themed room gone. All evidence, except that tell-tale feeling in his ass, gone.

He got dressed and slid into the car next to his cousin. "Can we go already? This place is creeping me out."

"What? Have another one of your alien abduction anal probe dreams again?"

No Cinnamon

T he snap of a cracking whip brought Liv back to her circumstances. A smile crossed her face. That had been good. So good she had blacked out.

"You still with me?" the deep voice of her master caressed her ears.

"Yes, Sir," she practically slurred in her blissed-out state.

"What's your safe word?" he asked.

"Cinnamon," she said.

"Good. Do you need to use it?"

"No, Sir. I'm good. I'm fucking amazing."

He chuckled. He may have even said something like, yes you are. But she was too blissed out to be aware. He was happy, she was happy. That's all that mattered.

She hung, too boneless to do much more than hold onto the chains that were cuffed to her wrists. She was in the center of a very specific type of playroom with walls full of toys. A large St. Andrews cross on one wall, bolts and chains and loops on another. She hung from the same loops that supported swings. With her hands positioned slightly above her head, she could lean on her wrists, but that was all the support, other than the floor under her feet, that she had. She swung around, feeling sweat and other things run down her legs, making her thighs slippery.

She closed her eyes when she felt her master's presence behind her. His body generated the slightest change in temperature. The room was already overly warm. Sweat ran beaded on her skin, running down between her breast, into the cleft of her ass.

When her master reached round, grasping and kneading her breasts, she leaned back into him. His cock was already hard again, and it prodded her.

Liv lifted her ass and tried to back up onto that desired appendage.

"Now, now," her master said, "did I say you could do that?"

"No," Liv pouted. "But I want it."

He cleared his throat, and the hands on her breast squeezed to the point of pain. She reveled in the sensations of it all. A long silence hovered between them as the pain grew in intensity.

"Sir," she finally said.

His hands eased, and the sensation of relief sharpened her nipples.

"Please, Sir, may I have it?"

"You ask very prettily, but I think you really want something else."

Not at all, she wanted his cock balls deep inside her cunt again. She wanted that vibrator up her ass. She wanted what he had just done to her. The last time he made her cum so hard she blacked out. That had never happened before, and she was going to be chasing that high again for a very long time.

His presence left her, she dangled alone. She twisted so she could see what he was doing. His back was to her, he was a tall, big man. Leather straps wrapped over his back and thighs. She had no clue what he looked like, he wore a leather mask.

It didn't matter what he looked like when he could make her feel the way he did.

She gasped when he reached for a flat paddle. She knew what that meant. When he turned back toward her, his cock was at full mast. She licked her lips, wanting it.

She arched her back as he approached. If she was good, if she didn't cry too much she would be rewarded. If she gave in and couldn't handle it anymore there would be no dick. And she was all about the dick.

The leather felt cool against her skin as her master began rubbing it over her hips and thighs.

She presented her ass. She gripped the chain and held herself still. If he landed the paddle just right he would smack her pussy, but she had to be in the right position or it wouldn't work.

The whir of the paddle moving through the air was her only warning before the leather landed with a crack.

She hissed. His aim had been off, and he caught more leg than was tolerable. He pulled on her hair, craning her neck, tipping her head back.

"What was that?" The voice that had been concerned and caring earlier now had its more familiar bite.

"Nothing, Sir." Liv could tell he was done being nice.

Biting the inside of her cheek with each smack, she would rather draw her own blood than to have him stop. Her ass was tender, and it burned. But she knew from experience, that burning sensation was what made the reward of cock all the more pleasurable. She also knew if she said cinnamon at any point, he wouldn't work with her again.

His cock, and the way he fucked was worth it, worth every second of it.

A moan escaped her, and the paddling stopped.

She sucked in a breath and held it. "Sorry, Sir. It's just so good I couldn't contain myself."

"Oh, you like that do you?"

"I like everything you do to me." She swallowed. "Sir." She wanted to yell at him to fuck her already. She wanted him to stop teasing her already and to fill her with jizz. She wanted all the pain so the pleasure would sing that much sweeter.

"I don't believe you." He slid a finger into her cunt.

She resisted the urge to sigh. His touch felt golden. Her muscles twitched and tried to grab at his fingers as he slid them out, and dragged them across her clit.

She thrust her hips out, following his fingers, longing for his touch to return.

"You do like what I do to you."

"Yes, Sir. I love it. I need it."

He took a step back and crossed his arms. "You can have it, if you can get it."

She pressed her hips out toward him, trying to find a way of touching him.

He laughed, but he stood his ground.

Liv grinned. She knew he thought she was weak. He hung her in the middle of the room for a reason. But he had underestimated her strength and determination. Readjusting her grip on the chain around her wrists, using her strength, she lifted herself straight up. She kicked her legs and swung out. She hooked her foot around his waist and dragged him closer as she wrapped her second leg around him. She sank down on his cock, and held his hips with her legs.

"You are determined," her master said, but he didn't uncross his arms or assist her in any way.

She had his cock now, and enough leverage. She pulsed against him, rocking her hips.

"Fuck it," he said. Finally, he wrapped his hands over her, digging his thick fingers into her skin. He began pulling her against him as he thrust forward.

Liv wanted to shout, she had what she wanted. Holding her chains she gripped him with her legs, holding him close as he pounded away. Her inner walls clenched down. She felt the glorious loss of all reason as she came around his cock, buried deep inside.

This time she didn't try to stifle her sounds. Her master was too invested now to stop and punish her. She reveled in the flashing lights behind her eyes, and the pounding that was between her legs. Her skin was on fire, and her ass burned even hotter from the paddling earlier. She was everything she wanted. She would live in this moment as long as she could. When the darkness came in around the edges, she laughed as she blacked out again.

Final Words

Hey it's Samantha Lexi; I hope you enjoyed these naughty short sex stories. The only way for me to know what type of particular stories you have enjoyed is by leaving an honest review on the product page, which will take less than 60 seconds of your time.

I will be able to create more tailored stories to your liking, and it will also help other readers discover these sexy intimate short stories!

Samantha Lexi x

CPSIA information can be obtained
at www.ICGtesting.com
Printed in the USA
BVHW041935200622
640233BV00006B/323

9 781915 470003